MR. FUSSY

by Roger Hargreaves

D0503431

Mr Fussy was fussy about everything.

Absolutely everything had to be neat and tidy and in its proper place.

Mr Fussy spent all day and every day rearranging his furniture, and making sure the flowers grew in a straight line in his garden, and trying to find specks of dust where there couldn't possibly be specks of dust because he spent all his time making sure there weren't any specks of dust.

One fine morning, Mr Fussy was having breakfast.

He was very fussy about what he ate.

He opened the marmalade pot.

"Ugh!" he exclaimed. "It's got bits in it!"

And he spent the rest of the morning separating the bits from the marmalade. Or, if you prefer, the marmalade from the bits.

"Fussy old fusspot" people used to call him.

Then Mr Fussy went out into his garden.

And spent the rest of the day straightening out all the blades of grass on his lawn!

Fussy old fusspot!

That evening Mr Fussy was in his kitchen (ironing his shoelaces) when he heard a crash outside.

"What's to do?" he murmured to himself, and hurried outside to investigate.

There, with a broken garden gate in one hand, an old battered suitcase in the other, and a sheepish grin on his face, stood an untidy person.

Mr Clumsy!

"Whoops!" he said, holding up the garden gate. "It came off in my hand!"

"Who," spluttered Mr Fussy, looking in horror at his garden gate, "are you?"

"I'm Mr Clumsy," replied the untidy person grinning, and he stepped forward to shake Mr Fussy's hand, but tripped over and fell on the lawn.

"My grass," cried Mr Fussy. "My straight grass. You've bent it!"

And he got down on his hands and knees, and started straightening the grass.

"But who are you?" he asked over his shoulder. "And why are you here?"

"I'm your cousin," replied Mr Clumsy. "Your long lost cousin from Australia. I've come to visit."

"Aren't you pleased to see me?" continued Mr Clumsy cheerfully, knocking over a flower or two as he got up, and picked up his suitcase, knocking over another flower or two, or three.

Mr Fussy, quite obviously, wasn't pleased to see him.

"You'd better come in," he muttered.

"I say," remarked Mr Clumsy, looking through the front door of Mr Fussy's house, "I say, what a neat little place you've got here!"

And he stepped inside, and tripped over his shoelaces (he often does), and knocked over a chair, and dropped his suitcase, and fell in an untidy heap on the floor.

"Whoops," he said.

Mr Fussy shut his eyes, and heaved a sigh, and groaned silently to himself.

Later that evening, after Mr Fussy had cooked them a meal, and after Mr Clumsy had helped with the washing up (two broken plates), they sat down to talk.

Mr Fussy sat, as he always did, in a neat and tidy fashion.

Mr Clumsy sat, as he always did, in a not so neat and tidy fashion.

"How long are you staying?" asked Mr Fussy.

"Oh, I don't know," grinned Mr Clumsy. "A few days. A week. A year. I haven't decided."

When he awoke in the morning, Mr Fussy jumped out of bed and went into his bathroom.

"Oh no," he gasped. "Oh no!"

Oh yes!

Mr Clumsy had been there before him.

The towels lay in a heap on the floor.

The bath was full of water.

There were pools of water all over the bathroom floor, and, half a tube of toothpaste!

What a mess!

Mr Fussy made it all neat and tidy as quickly as he could.

Then Mr Fussy hurried downstairs.

"Morning," said his cousin cheerfully. "I've cooked you breakfast. Sit down!"

There was an awful mess everywhere.

"There we are," said Mr Clumsy, carrying a plate of fried eggs (broken fried eggs) towards the table. "Breakfast!"

And then he tripped over those shoelaces of his, and then the eggs flew through the air, and then they landed all over Mr Fussy.

Sticky, greasy, yellow, fried eggs!

"Whoops," said Mr Clumsy.

After a week, Mr Fussy's house didn't look like Mr Fussy's house any more at all.

But, after two weeks, Mr Clumsy decided to move on.

"Thank you for having me," he said to Mr Fussy.

"It was very nice to see you," replied Mr Fussy politely.

But what he was thinking was, "It's very nice to see you going."

"Cheerio," said Mr Clumsy, and off he went with his battered old suitcase.

"Goodbye," called Mr Fussy, really meaning, "Good riddance!"

Then Mr Fussy fussed around his house as he'd never fussed before.

Fussy old fusspot!

Polishing, and mending, and repairing, and straightening, and sorting out, and cleaning, and putting everything back exactly as it had been before Mr Clumsy had come to stay.

He even dusted the flowers in the garden!

That evening Mr Fussy was in his kitchen (polishing an egg) when he heard a crash outside.

"Oh no," he groaned. "Not Mr Clumsy back again. It can't be! It mustn't be! It isn't!"

And it wasn't!

It was somebody else.

Somebody who had just walked straight through Mr Fussy's garden gate.

Somebody who can't help having little accidents.

Somebody you may have met before.

"Hello," smiled Mr Bump.

"I've come to visit!"

Fantastic offers for Mr. Men fans!

Collect all your Mr. Men or Little Miss books in these superb durable collectors' cases!
Only £5.99 inc. postage and packing, these wipe-clean, hard-wearing cases will give all your Mr. Men or Little Miss books a beautiful new home!

Keep track of your collection with this giant-sized double-sided Mr. Men and Little Miss Collectors' poster.
Collect 6 tokens and we will send you a brilliant giant-sized double-sided collectors' poster! Simply tape a £1 coin to cover postage and packaging in the space provided and fill out the form overleaf.

Only need a few Mr. Men or Little Miss to complete your set? You can order any of the titles on the back of the books from our Mr. Men order line on 0870 787 1724. Orders should be delivered between 5 and 7 working days.

--- **TO BE COMPLETED BY AN ADULT** ---

To apply for any of these great offers, ask an adult to complete the details below and send this whole page with the appropriate payment and tokens, to: MR. MEN CLASSIC OFFER, PO BOX 715, HORSHAM RH12 5WG

☐ Please send me a giant-sized double-sided collectors' poster.
AND ☐ I enclose 6 tokens and have taped a £1 coin to the other side of this page.

☐ Please send me ☐ Mr. Men Library case(s) and/or ☐ Little Miss library case(s) at £5.99 each inc P&P

☐ I enclose a cheque/postal order payable to Egmont UK Limited for £...............

OR ☐ Please debit my MasterCard / Visa / Maestro / Delta account (delete as appropriate) for £...............

Card no. ☐☐☐☐ ☐☐☐☐ ☐☐☐☐ ☐☐☐☐ ☐☐☐☐ Security code ☐☐☐

Issue no. (if available) ☐ Start Date ☐☐/☐☐/☐☐ Expiry Date ☐☐/☐☐/☐☐

Fan's name: .... Date of birth: ....

Address: ....

....

.... Postcode: ....

Name of parent / guardian: ....

Email for parent / guardian: ....

Signature of parent / guardian: ....

Please allow 28 days for delivery. Offer is only available while stocks last. We reserve the right to change the terms of this offer at any time and we offer a 14 day money back guarantee. This does not affect your statutory rights. Offers apply to UK only.

☐ We may occasionally wish to send you information about other Egmont children's books. If you would rather we didn't, please tick this box.

Ref: MRM 001